Much Ado About Muffin

The Mysteries of Cozy Cove
Book 1

Virginia K. Bennett

*To Virginia Cantara, Barbara Keenan and
Gilly Bennett, the grandmothers who were fiercely ahead
of their time and gave me my name.
Thank you for being authentically you!*

I love you!

Table of Contents

Chapter 1

License to Grill

MACKENZIE AND LUCAS WALKED ALONG THE FIRM beach sand where the waves almost touched their shoes. It was still too early in the year to take them off and walk in the water, hence the pants and jackets on both of them. This being only a first date, and probably the last based on the body language, they were not holding hands. The dinner conversation had been forced, mainly focusing on Lucas's love of sci-fi movies and his plans for the next Comic-Con event in Boston. He kept telling Mackenzie about the cosplay costumes he planned to create because he wouldn't be caught dead wearing the same one multiple days.

He was very proud of his Luke Sky-Walker Texas Ranger concept but thought maybe he would lead off with Marty McFly. When she asked if he would be wearing the life preserver vest, he nearly spit out his drink. "No one who knows anything about Comic-Con would show up in that outfit. Everyone would know they were a first-timer." Apparently, being a first-timer was a very bad thing to be accused of according to Lucas who happened to have a similar build and haircut to Michael J. Fox. "No, I'd wear the 1955 outfit when he goes back to his high school in the two-tone leather jacket. That would turn heads." Mackenzie decided to smile and nod then returned to chewing her food.

The walk was not providing them with any more conversation inspiration, even with the stunning scenery and reflection of the moon off the surface of the ocean. Mackenzie was starting to realize that a late night out on a Saturday was not a good plan, considering she still had to get up for work early Sunday morning. Ahead of them, something was moving in the water. At first, they assumed it was something like seaweed or debris that had washed up on the beach from the ocean but as they got closer, it was clear that the large lump was not something that came naturally from the surf.

Mackenzie started running first. She approached the pile on the ground and realized it was a body, lying prone, being pulled down and back up the sand by the ebb and flow of the waves. Once Lucas caught up, they both began working to flip the person over.

"Is he breathing?" Mackenzie quickly inhaled and exhaled around the words then let out a gasp and covered her mouth.

"I don't think so. Is there a pulse?"

Lucas grabbed for a wrist while Mackenzie hesitated before putting two fingers to the neck. Fifteen seconds passed before either took their next breath. Feeling no movement, Mackenzie started removing clothing, looking for an injury, while Lucas dropped his ear to the chest of what they now believed to be the deceased body of a middle-aged man. Lucas still had no evidence to support life, including both the color and state of the skin, so he grabbed his phone from his back pocket and dialed 9-1-1.

When Mackenzie opened the flaps of the unbuttoned jacket on the body, she found a large rip in the shirt underneath. Pulling up the shirt revealed a large gash in the skin, but only diluted staining on the shirt and inside of the jacket. Based on the rest of the body and fabric, evidence would suggest any blood that might have originated in the wound, when the injury happened, had now been washed away by the salt water. Standing over the body, Lucas spoke to the 9-1-1 operator in a surprisingly calm manner via speaker phone.

"9-1-1, what's your emergency?"

"Yeah, I was just walking along the beach with my... date...and we found a body. A dead guy. He was in the water. In the ocean."

"Is the person breathing? Is there a pulse?"

"No. Nothing. We both checked for a pulse and breathing, and nothing."

"What is your location?"

"The beach. Just east of Cozy Cove. We're at the end where the river drains. Can you send someone, please?"

"I'm contacting police and rescue now. Please stay on the line."

"Okay."

He held the phone in front of him, waiting for an

update, but they heard the sirens long before the operator told them what was happening. Cozy Cove and the surrounding towns had one central Police and Fire Station that covered them all, so it would be a short wait for the sirens to be right at the edge of the sand.

Mackenzie was quite cold now as kneeling in the surf got everything wet below her waist. The slight breeze made her body temperature fall that much faster. What once was a perfect blowout of stunning red hair was now a matted mess due to the moisture in the air and splashing that occurred during the last five or so minutes. The police officers offered their cars to wait in while EMTs raced down the beach with a long spine board and bags of supplies they wouldn't need. Lucas was put in a different car from Mackenzie – standard practice when police needed to interview suspects or witnesses. They both knew what happened, but the police would need to sort that out by seeing that their stories matched.

Almost an hour later, Lucas and Mackenzie were released and sent on their way with a request to stay in the area and to be prepared for follow-up questioning by state troopers. Business cards were given to each of them with contact numbers should they think of anything else once they left the scene. Mackenzie looked back over her shoulder as the EMTs were loading the long spine board carrying the body into the back of the ambulance.

"Lucas, I can't believe he's dead."

"Who? The victim? Of course he's dead. We both determined that."

"No, I mean the person. I can't believe he's dead. I just saw him this morning."

"Who? You saw *who* this morning? You know the victim?"

"Don't you? You saw the jacket when we got to the body to flip him over. It was Bobby. Bobby Porter."

- Two Hours Earlier -

"And the winner of the Grilling Association of Southern Maine trophy for Best Griller of the Year is ... Bobby Porter of Porter's Steak House."

A handsome man in his early forties leapt to the stage, two steps at a time, the smile on his face stretching from ear to ear. Already on stage were three other infamous grillers from the area who all expected to win themselves. Bobby first shook hands and did a half-hug and back slap with the third runner-up, Henry York. Being the heavy-set man of only about five and a half feet with a thatch of white hair atop his head that he was, Henry posed as the gracious loser while he received the hug-and-slap motion from the excited winner. As Bobby moved on, Chef York rolled his eyes and sneered in the opposite direction.

Brandy Kelly was the next chef to receive the elation radiating from Bobby's every cell. He shook her hand then pulled her in for a full hug that lifted her onto her toes. Ever the feminist, she looked perturbed that she didn't receive either the same treatment as Henry or something similar. Her hands smoothed the front of her pantsuit with frustration though the identical braids on either side of her face remained unaffected by the gesture. She couldn't even muster a smile as he held her shoulders in his two meaty hands.

The final and, by all accounts, angriest-looking human on the planet was the first runner-up, Mark Dunn. The owner and head chef of a steakhouse just up the road from Porter's was not even attempting to hide his rage at finishing behind Bobby. A long beat passed as Bobby held out a hand, waiting for Mark to grasp it. When the handshake never came, Bobby clapped Mark on one shoulder and slid over to the host who was holding the coveted trophy out for the winner.

"Congratulations, Bobby. What's the first thing you will do now that you've won Griller of the Year?"

Bobby appeared to be a bit choked up. He stood behind the podium and brought his face close to the microphone.

"I am going to invite my fellow grillers over to Porter's to share a steak dinner cooked by the best griller in southern Maine!"

With that, Bobby held his new trophy high above his head and backed away from the podium. The three chefs to his right seethed with fake smiles firmly placed in front of their anger as Bobby strutted over to them for the official photographer to take a picture that would be featured above the fold of tomorrow's Sunday edition of the So-Me Times.

"Everyone, please look this way." The eager photographer waved at the quartet to maintain their attention long enough to get a usable photo of the group. "Before you leave, can I please get your names and places of business for the paper?"

"Why don't you just get it from the organizers?" spat Mark. "It's not like you can't do your own research." Clearly, Mark wasn't done being upset just yet.

"His name is Mark Dunn, and he owns 'Well Dunn' spelled D-U-N-N. You know, like a play on a well-done steak. That must be the most creative steakhouse name ever, if you ask me." Brandy's sarcasm oozed from the way she spoke the sentence. "I'm Brandy Kelly, and I own Respect the Skirt just north of here. It's not easy being a female chef or grill master in a male-dominated industry."

"Yeah, well, if you want to gain respect in this industry you need to earn it." Mark's charm was, well, completely absent tonight.

"You do know we both lost to Bobby, right?" Hands on her hips, she waited for his witty response.

"Well, I still beat you. More than Henry can say." Mark smiled for the first time since the runners-up had been announced. "What say you, Sir Henry?"

"I may not have won the competition, but at least I'm not a poxy of a man like you, Mark. You're a right prat, you are."

7

"Guys, guys...and lady. What are we getting on about?" Bobby decided to step in as the father-figure of the group. Yes, he had won today, but over the years there had been many different winners, several with now failed restaurants. Winning Griller of the Year was not a stamp guaranteeing future success. The way this group was going on, it would make an outside observer think Bobby was holding an Oscar.

"Bobby, you have a restaurant that serves steak and baked potatoes, and everyone loves you. The last thing your ego needed was an award that implied your restaurant was better than any of ours." Mark was right about Porter's. They served a variety of cuts of meat, grilled to your preferred temperature, with a small list of sides to choose from that never deviated from the opening-day menu. And no one bothered asking for a vegetarian or vegan option – the garden salad was the only choice that wasn't fish, meat, cooked with meat or covered in some byproduct of an animal. "Winning this award doesn't give you the right to be a jerk for the next year."

"I'll just have to win next year too so I can be a jerk two years in a row." Below the stage, the photographer continued to snap candids and jot notes feverishly. "Don't forget to write in your article that I plan to win next year as well."

Bobby Porter had lived in and around Cozy Cove, Maine, for his whole life. He attended the same schools as both of his parents and permanently returned from the University of New Hampshire with his B.S. in Hotel and Hospitality Management after four years. During college, he accrued over four hundred hours of on-the-job experience in all aspects of management that he put to good use helping with the steakhouse that had already been in the family for three generations. After training under his father to become a grill master, he had taken over the kitchen so his parents could retire. Bobby had only been in charge for a couple of years before winning the coveted title of griller of the year.

He posed for a few more photos, all in his trademark jean jacket covered in patches. Bobby was always seen either wearing that or his apron if he was grilling. A product of the eighties, Bobby still listened to hair band icons like Cinderella, Def Leopard, Bon Jovi and Mötley Crüe in his kitchen. Turning for the camera, he posed with his collar flipped up and the Porter's Steak House logo prominently featured on the back of the jacket.

As he sauntered from the stage, he called over his shoulder, "You don't know what you've got, 'til it's gone."

"He's livin' on a prayer is what he is," stated Mark.

"Nah." Brandy shook her head. "Wanted dead or alive is more like it."

"He's going out in a blaze of glory," Henry scoffed.

All three looked at each other and chuckled. Before departing, the photographer commented, "Someone should take him down a peg. He gives grilling a bad name."

Chapter 2

Muffin Can Stop Me Now

"GOOD MORNING, ARTHUR."

A man in his seventies, with hair and skin that did not agree with his chronological age but in a good way, reentered the bakery through swinging saloon doors behind the counter. He finished adjusting his apron just as the customer approached the glass. Arthur's kind nature shown brilliantly across his face as he waited on the customer. "What can I get for you this fine Sunday morning, Phyllis?"

"I'll have one of those snickerdoodle muffin tops. I know it's really a glorified cookie, but they're so good!" Phyllis happened to only show up when Arthur worked at the bakery and always waited until he was behind the counter with his apron firmly affixed to order her muffin, or muffin top on this occasion.

"No problem. Anything else for you?"

"That will be all. Thank you." Phyllis placed some cash on the counter and accepted her napkin-wrapped treat from Arthur. She let out a small giggle when their hands touched as he handed her the change and smiled.

"Arthur," Mackenzie proclaimed. "I'm heading into the back to bake some more cranberry-orange muffin tops. Will you just holler if you need me out here?"

"Sure thing, Mac."

Mackenzie Walsh was the owner and head baker at Top O' the Muffin to Ya, a small bakery conveniently located in the center of Cozy Cove, Maine. Arthur checked to see which apron she wore today – Ya Bakin' Me Crazy. Mackenzie was not only the head baker; she was the *only* baker. Her work ethic was second to none, which is probably why she and Arthur made such a great pair. She arrived at the bakery each morning by 3:30am to get started on the goodies for that day. As a responsible member of the community, she donated any unpurchased goods to the family shelter in the next town over. A scone baked in the morning was certainly fine come the next, but she didn't feel right charging her loyal customers for day-old pastries. The shelter had obviously accepted the donations and thanked her profusely every chance they got.

"Before you go, why couldn't the teddy bear finish his muffin?"

"I don't know. Why?" Mackenzie and Arthur danced this dance each morning. She couldn't believe that he was still coming up with baked-good jokes and puns she hadn't already heard. He must be really good at Googling.

"Because he was stuffed."

She chuckled at this one before retreating to the sanctuary that was her kitchen. It was a much better response than yesterday when he asked what bakers give women on special occasions. Arthur was so proud of his joke that he had to force himself to stop laughing before he could tell her the correct response was *flours*. Mackenzie was so distracted by mundane work tasks when he told her that she didn't get it. "Don't lots of men give flowers to women?" Arthur walked through the saloon doors and returned with a measuring cup full of flour, pointing to it straight-faced.

"Gotcha." She must have been *really* distracted because she rarely missed a joke, especially a baking joke, and typically humored the older gentleman.

She was distracted for an entirely different reason this morning. Last night, she and her first-and-only-time date, Lucas, discovered the body of prominent local chef Bobby Porter abandoned on the shore of Dogwood Beach. She and Lucas had been questioned by police and released with the caveat that there would probably be more questions coming as the investigation moved on. She had been so focused on the bakery this morning, she hadn't even been able to update Arthur on what happened.

After several customers and about twenty-five minutes, Arthur poked his head into the kitchen. "Mac, there are two state troopers here to see you. Everything okay?" The pinched brows and extra wrinkles on Arthur's face told her that he was very concerned.

"Yes. I'll be right out. And yes, everything is okay

with me." She brushed off the flour from her hands, washed them and walked to the front of the shop.

"Ms. Mackenzie Walsh, is that correct?" asked a petite trooper with the name Zhào on the pin above her right breast pocket.

"Yes, I am she." Mackenzie stepped out from behind the counter to shake hands with both officers.

"I'm State Trooper Linda Zhào, and this is my partner, State Trooper Matthew Smith."

"Good morning. Would you like something to eat or drink?"

"No, thank you. We're all set."

"Well," Trooper Smith interjected, "I wouldn't turn down a pastry."

"Your choice. What'll you have?"

Trooper Smith looked ready to drool at the array of options. Since it was early enough in the morning, most of the favorites were still available.

"I'd love anything with cinnamon and sugar."

"I've got it," stated Arthur. He grabbed a crumb coffee cake muffin top from the case, wrapped it in a napkin, and handed it over the domed glass to Trooper Smith.

"Thank you." He began to eat it immediately, leaving the talking to Trooper Zhào.

"Ms. Walsh, were you the one who discovered the body of Bobby Porter last night at Dogwood Beach?" At this, Arthur gasped.

"Mackenzie, you didn't tell me that."

"I didn't have time. You just got here, and we were busy. Sorry. Yes, I did, along with my date."

"We just wanted to see if you remembered anything else from last night. Anything you didn't already tell the local officers."

Mackenzie put real thought into her answer. She had told them about the position of the body when they found it, conditions of the skin and face, the damage to the shirt and lack of blood...nothing else came to mind. "I can't think of anything I didn't already tell them. The wound, however, still strikes me as off. There was quite an opening, but not a clean tear. I'm not sure how else to describe it. No blood, presumably washed away, but such a strange opening because it didn't really look like a cut. And there was nothing lying around that looked like it could have made the wound, but I suppose anything could have been in the water. I'm sure that doesn't help, but I felt like I should say it."

"Thank you, Ms. Walsh. We have a team looking into all of those details and appreciate your efforts last night." Trooper Zhào checked on Trooper Smith who was finishing up his muffin top. She had previously learned her lesson and was not letting him back in the cruiser with that crumb creator.

"Yes, and thank you for the breakfast." Trooper Smith wiped his mouth before disposing of the napkin. "It was delicious."

"We'll be heading out, but here is my card in case you need to reach us or think of anything else." Trooper Zhào handed a card to Mackenzie and headed out the door, followed by Trooper Smith.

Absentmindedly, Mackenzie stared at the card as she turned and walked back to the kitchen, followed by Arthur.

"Apparently there is a lot that we need to talk about, young lady," scolded Arthur. Before he could dig any further, he immediately returned to the front of the shop as he heard the tinkle of a bell, alerting them to a customer entering or leaving. His military crew cut still perfectly trimmed, Arthur was the model employee: always arrived on time, always performed his duties to the best of his ability and always faithful. If someone came in complaining, Arthur politely stood up for the shop, and Mackenzie, but made sure they left feeling heard and compensated. He did believe the customer was always right, but that didn't mean he wouldn't go to the back later to tell Mackenzie what he really thought about them. Mackenzie, however, would come out from the back like a momma bear if needed. She was the owner and was more than capable of telling a customer their business was not welcome if they were not going to treat her Arthur in a respectful manner. They balanced each other well.

"Good morning, Arthur."

"Yes, good morning, Arthur." Every Sunday, Michael and Michael, the Michaels, entered the shop ready to sit at a table and sip drinks, chat and order more than one round of pastries. Original Michael, who grew up in Cozy Cove, was a special education teacher and one of the sweetest men you ever met. Michael Number Two, though no one ever said that to his face, moved here after meeting Original Michael in a drag bar. He was performing as Dare-I-Go, a play on the state seal featuring the word DIRIGO, meaning 'I lead' in Latin. And as mother of the House of Boots, it was the perfect drag name for a queen in Maine.

"Good morning, Michaels. How was last night?" Arthur was asking about the drag show in town that Dare-I-Go performed in every Saturday night; Friday nights were reserved for shows outside of the local area – Boston, Portland and the occasional New York City gig.

"Went just fine, as always."

"He's being modest. It was a stellar night where he hosted and sang, twice!" Always his biggest supporter, Original Michael pumped up his partner's ego whenever possible.

"What can I get you two?" Arthur started moving cups and grabbing for the tea options as the order very rarely deviated from a couple reliable choices.

"You choose this morning. We trust you. We'll just be over here, okay?" Michael Number Two pointed to an empty table by the window.

"Be there in a minute." Arthur went with green tea for Original Michael and black tea for Michael Number Two; he was looking a little low on energy. A small serving of cream and sugars were added to the platter along with one cranberry-orange muffin top and a plain scone. Arthur enjoyed a challenge and watched for the reactions on both faces as he approached their table.

"Perfect. Absolutely perfect. Do we come here too often, Arthur?"

"Not according to Mackenzie and me. We'd love to see you more than just Sundays."

"Well, don't you worry. As soon as school is out, I'll be here more often, just like every summer."

"Arthur," whispered Michael Number Two. He angled his body closer to Arthur, and Arthur dropped lower, closer to Michael's face. "Did you hear about Bobby?"

"You didn't hear it from me, but Mackenzie is the one who discovered the body last night."

"Oh, that poor girl."

"I don't know any more than that right now, but I'm keeping a close eye on her today. What have you heard?"

"Just that he won some award last night and now he's dead. The award was the headline on the paper this morning. No mention of the murder, but rumors started immediately."

"We heard about it when we stopped at the grocery store before coming here." Original Michael knew everyone, having lived here his whole life and working in education, there wasn't a student, parent or similarly aged community member that Michael couldn't or wouldn't start up a conversation with. "Please, do watch out for Mackenzie. We worry about her, still single, you know."

Placing his hands in the front pockets of his waist apron, Arthur reported, "I'm taking her out to dinner tonight to make sure she's not alone and find out what happened. She's in good hands."

"Good to know. Thank you, Arthur."

The rest of the day went by uneventfully. Mackenzie worked in the back for most of it, unless things got too busy up front. She swiftly rescued Arthur a few times and then disappeared back to the kitchen, trying to keep up with demand. The bakery closed up for the day at 2pm, and so began the cleaning process. They were closed Mondays, so an extensive deep clean was performed before leaving on Sundays.

"Arthur, you can go if you want. I'll clean up. You worked quite the full day."

"Mackenzie, how many times do I have to tell you. I enjoy working. I enjoy feeling useful. Working for you is a lot like having a drill sergeant back when I was in Vietnam." He chuckled at the reaction he got. Her eyebrows shot up to her matching copper-colored hairline, and her jaw nearly hit the counter.

"I...what do you...how am I..."

"I'm just kidding. You know how much I love having a purpose, and working with you has been great since Charlotte passed away."

Arthur had the kindest and toughest soul, hardened from years in the military. He had several active-duty deployments, more than enough stamps in his passport and decades of love and laughter with Charlotte. When she passed away a few years ago, he didn't know what to do with himself. There weren't enough projects around the house to keep him busy. He'd been retired for so many years now, he'd done them all, and some more than once. When he found himself too lonely at home, he started walking and exploring all of the shops and eateries in and around Cozy Cove.

One morning, Arthur ordered a coffee and blueberry muffin from Mackenzie after a long wait in a line that went out the door. It was a Saturday morning, so busier than week days, but she was working alone. He had never watched someone hustle the way she did. At the conclusion of his coffee and muffin, he cleared his table and tidied up the others that had been left in disarray. Most customers were just picking up things to go, so he continued to occupy a table in the corner. As patrons came and went from the tables, he continued to attend to the ones that needed attending.

After a long sigh around 1:30pm, the hustler behind the counter introduced herself. "Hey, I'm Mackenzie, but most people just call me Mac. Thanks so much for your help today. Can I send you home with some pastries or give you a gift card?"

"Absolutely not, but I'd love to have a job. Are you hiring?" It was the strangest attempt at organizing his own interview, but he was going to run with it as he stood and approached the counter.

"Well, I'm kind of in the spot I'm in because I can't afford to pay as much as other shops and the tips aren't great, other than during the tourist season."

"Good thing I work cheap. I'm retired with time on my hands. I'm a good employee and need something to do. If it doesn't work out, it'll be easy to fire me." He could see the wheels turning behind her emerald eyes. She did need some help. He seemed nice enough and clearly wasn't deterred by her glowing description of what she had to offer. "I will stop at muffin to help you succeed." That did it.

"I'm open Tuesday through Sunday. I really need the help on Saturday and Sunday the most if you are available on the weekends. I really can't afford to pay you more than ten hours per week, so maybe just the busiest times from eight to one?"

"How about I guarantee I'll be here from eight to one every Saturday and Sunday. If I feel like volunteering any other times, you'll let me and not force me to take payment other than snacks." They stared at each other for a long beat, sizing each other up. Mackenzie was a formidable five foot eight where Arthur was a hunched five foot ten. At one point in his life he might have been six feet, but after seventy plus years on this earth, he was a bit shorter.

"It's a deal." Mackenzie's arm reached across the counter for a firm handshake.

"Mac, I'll see you tomorrow by 8am." And with that, Arthur turned and walked to the front double doors of the bakery, opening and holding the door for a customer trying to sneak in before she closed. The origin story of their friendship was quite unique, but it didn't stop there.

Arthur showed up that Sunday morning just after seven. He didn't know what someone wore to work at a bakery, so he went with comfortable shoes, pants and a short-sleeved button-up shirt, bringing a cardigan draped over his arm just in case he got cold but didn't think he would need it. Arriving an hour before the busy time seemed reasonable enough, but clearly, she was trying to be as strategic as possible with her ten hours. The line was already out the door, and she was busy behind the register.

"Excuse me. Excuse me." Arthur politely passed by patrons waiting in line giving him the side-eye. "I'm here. How can I help?"

"Wash your hands and throw on an apron. I'll tell you what to grab from the case. Plates are behind you and wax paper is under the case with the paper bags to go." That was Arthur's training. He learned on the job over the course of the morning and early afternoon. His first day was a Sunday, and so began the deep cleaning process once the doors were locked up.

"Wow, Arthur. You were more help than I ever could have hoped for. Take whatever you want home with you, and I'll see you Saturday. Thank you so much."

"Mac, what will you do now?"

"It's Sunday. I'll clean for a few hours because I'm not open on Monday."

"Then I'll clean too. I'd hate for you to do it all on your own if you don't need to."

Mackenzie might have been the owner, but it was clear that Arthur was going to be the boss of this new friendship. "I'd love the help and the company. Why don't you tell me more about your wife."

"Arthur. Arthur? Are you okay?" Mackenzie broke the dream-like memory of the first time she and Arthur met by shaking him on the shoulder. "Arthur, what's wrong?"

"Oh, nothing. I was just remembering about when we first met."

"Best deal I ever agreed to," she said with a wink.

"I was wondering if you wanted to have dinner with me tonight. We have tomorrow off, and I don't want to cook for just me. My treat, and I'll pick you up."

"You drive a hard bargain, offering to take me out to dinner. I'm in. Where and when?"

"Let's eat at Porter's Steak House. I called during a break to see if they are still open, and they are. I was shocked. What do you think?"

Mackenzie didn't know what to think; because of that she said, "Yes. I'm curious how they are open and what's going on there."

"If we get there and it's too awkward, we can go somewhere else, okay?"

"Sure. Pick me up at six? Gives me enough time to go home, shower and put something clean on. I can't stand having my hair up all night after working like this all day."

"Yea, same here." They both chuckled, finished cleaning and packed up to leave for their respective homes. Arthur was walking toward his car while Mackenzie locked up. "Remember, I'm muffin without you!"

Chapter 3

There's a Lot at Steak

ARTHUR DROVE TO MACKENZIE'S HOUSE, WITH A perfectly clean driving record. He pulled up outside of her house at 5:57pm. She had inherited her home from her grandmother; that's how she ended up in Cozy Cove to begin with. Her grandmother, Grammy B, had always loved Cozy Cove and the surrounding coastline. When she retired, she bought small homes in both Maine and Florida. From early May through late October, Grammy B lived at 13 Birch Tree Lane, so named because the whole street was lined with mature birch trees on both sides. The rest of the year, Grammy B migrated south to a gated retirement community. The two-bedroom, single-story box in Florida was a house, but the property in Cozy Cove was her home.

Mackenzie would forever be grateful for her grand-mother's foresight. She left the home on Birch Tree Lane to Mac, free and clear, when she passed away almost ten years ago. It was hard for Mackenzie to believe it had already been that long. Because of the home, Mackenzie could afford to save her money and eventually live her dream of owning a bakery. A small ice cream shop closed down in the best possible location in the center of Cozy Cove. As soon as rumors of the impending closure started flying, Mackenzie swooped in to make an offer. Due to the amount of cash she had saved up, she was able to purchase the location and not just rent it. Her determination and hustle came down to the fact that she had everything to lose if this gamble wasn't a success. Arthur showed up at just the right time in her life when the coin could have flipped either way.

Knock, knock, knock. Mackenzie answered the door in a simple, cap-sleeved dress that stopped just below the knee. "Come in. Let me grab my jacket and we're off." Arthur, ever the gentleman, stepped just inside but stayed on the mat as to not get her floors dirty; Charlotte would be proud.

"You look lovely, Miss Mackenzie."

"Arthur, you keep calling me Miss like I didn't pass forty years ago."

"Well, you're younger than I am, so Miss it will be until you marry."

"And what if I never marry?" Mackenzie didn't know if she ever would but still held out hope her Mr. Right was out there somewhere. She wouldn't have time to get to know him or fall in love, but maybe he'd just fall into her lap, like Arthur.

"I believe he's out there. Until then, you're Miss Mackenzie when you get all dressed up like that."

They shared a sweet moment. He needed her just as much as she needed him.

"And in the bakery, it's Drill Sargent Walsh to you, soldier." She couldn't sound mean if she wanted to...not to Arthur. She grabbed a jacket off the edge of the couch.

"Shall we head out?" He offered her his arm and walked her to the passenger side of his car, opening the door for her. Not surprisingly, it was a practical Volvo – nothing flashy, but safe and good in the Maine winters. Arthur had opted not to become a snowbird. He devoted most of his free time to helping Mackenzie in the bakery and playing the role of pseudo-grandfather.

Once inside the car, Mackenzie turned to Arthur. "What's the deal? State Troopers reveal that I found the body of Bobby Porter and suddenly you want to take me out to Porter's for dinner. What aren't you telling me?"

Arthur tried to look innocent, but she knew him too well. He only attempted to fake it for about thirty seconds. "Well, I thought it was strange that the Michaels said Bobby's death didn't make the papers but his grilling award did. I called the steakhouse to see if they were open today because I was curious. When the hostess answered and said they were open for dinner, I had about a dozen questions flood my mind. Taking you out to dinner seemed like it killed two birds with one stone, if you'll excuse the poorly timed expression."

Mackenzie knew this was all truth because Arthur couldn't lie to her. She watched him lie to just about everyone else one way or another, but not her. Guilt splashed across his face like a neon sign when he tried, though he didn't try often. He even spoiled her surprise party last year because he couldn't pull it off. "Which two birds will it kill?"

"Making sure you aren't alone tonight and looking into the details of an open restaurant of the now deceased eponymous owner of the conveniently timed, award-winning steakhouse."

"Wow, you really thought that through."

"Actually, I was hoping the dinner might help you. I didn't know if you needed closure."

Arthur was thoughtful like that. He was concerned about his friend and wanted to support her any way he could. He even offered to not go there if it made her feel uncomfortable.

"Let's go. I do want to find out what's going on. How are they even open without their head chef? Who's in charge now? Good thinking, Arthur." She gave him a slug on his right shoulder, a light one, and buckled her seat belt.

Arriving at the steakhouse only a few minutes later, they had to take the one and only road that led into Cozy Cove from the adjoining town. By car, there was only one way in and that same way out. It did cause traffic issues during the busy summer months, but October through April it wasn't much of an issue. Mackenzie took the footbridge that connected the peninsula, most recognized as Cozy Cove, to the "mainland" part of town on her way to and from work each day. Because Porter's was at the end of the peninsula, further down than her bakery, and because Arthur was picking her up, they needed to actually drive out of the town of Cozy Cove, into Dogwood, and back into Cozy Cove.

On a Sunday night, parking wasn't too difficult. The peninsula was pretty cramped, so other times of the year or week could be tricky. They walked from the car to the front door, where Arthur proceeded to open it for Mackenzie, and up to the hostess podium. "Table for two under the name Arthur."

"Of course, right this way, Arthur." A tall blonde escorted them to a table near the front of the restaurant, not the back where the floor to ceiling windows provided epic views of the ocean.

"Excuse me, Miss, but who is the chef tonight? So sorry to hear about Bobby."

"Yes, tonight's chef is Jason Bell, the sous chef to Bobby for about the last year."

Mackenzie chimed in next. "And if you don't mind me asking, who is running things with Bobby gone?"

The hostess was taken aback. She looked as if this question had earnestly surprised her. "Oh, well, his family met with Jason and me this morning. We expressed that it would be best for all of Bobby's employees to stay open, if possible, until big decisions could be made regarding ownership and control of the restaurant. Jason and I volunteered to run things as Bobby would have until they were done with funeral arrangements and such so bills and staff could continue to get paid. That is, as long as customers are still coming." She shuffled her feet and looked down at them. Around her eyes appeared to be puffy and the whites of her eyes bloodshot.

"Again, we're so sorry for your loss. Please accept our condolences." Mackenzie felt badly now for prodding.

"Of course, and thank you. Your waiter will be here in a moment." The tall blonde headed back to the podium.

"We need to remember to write up our review on Yelp or Facebook to help out," Mackenzie suggested.

Arthur was already searching the menu. "I'm sorry, what was that?"

"Oh, nothing. What are you going to get?"

They participated in small talk about the bakery and the weather between ordering and eating. Nothing was of particular importance until it seemed the night was winding down. "Mac, are you doing okay? Finding a dead body, regardless of whose body it is, is not something to just blow off. If you need to talk about it, to me or to a therapist, please do."

She balled up her cloth napkin and placed it on the table. "I am doing surprisingly well. I know that I did everything I could and that he was already gone before we found him. Now, we'll just have to see what can be done about finding his killer."

"Do you think there is a killer? Is there any chance this was just a horrible accident?"

Before she could answer, the waiter stopped by to see if they were finished or would like some dessert. Arthur accepted the bill, scanned it and handed the black folder back to the waiter with his credit card. The waiter shuffled off to settle up the table.

Voice lowered, Mackenzie spoke as if she were giving someone her secret frosting recipe. "There is no way that wound was an accident. It was big and not caused by rocks. There was nothing else around him to be used as a weapon, and there was no weapon in the wound."

"What makes you so sure it wasn't caused by a rock? What if he was drunk and wandered into the water and fell on something. Or, what if he fell before he got down to the beach and just kept walking toward the water before losing too much blood and passing out?" Arthur seemed confident in his hypotheses.

"There was no blood left anywhere, only staining on his clothes. None on the sand around him. If he wasn't killed in the water, he was right next to it for the surf to wash it away."

"And why couldn't he have fallen on a rock?" Arthur questioned.

"What does it look like when *you* fall on a rock?" Mackenzie asked, inquisitively.

"Lots of scrapes and cuts around a larger bruise or significant cut.

"Right, and that significant cut, is it smooth and clean?"

"No, probably not." Arthur's once confident face now showed that he could tell where she was going.

The waiter unobtrusively dropped off the black folder so Arthur could sign the slip and – hopefully – leave a tip.

"Exactly. This wound was weird. Clean. No signs of scrapes or other cuts. Maybe starting to bruise around it, but that could have been from the water or cold temperature. I've never seen someone get stabbed, but it didn't look like what I would imagine a stabbing to result in."

"So, it sounds like you too are curious about the circumstances around this death. Let's get some sleep and we can chat about it Tuesday morning while we're opening the shop."

Mackenzie nodded and they both stood, having remembered to sign the credit card slip before leaving the table. Just before exiting the front door, a framed newspaper article caught her eye.

"Arthur, they certainly got this framed quickly. Who do you think made sure this was done before starting service tonight." Perfectly matted and framed, a newspaper clipping from the previous night was hanging to the left of the front door.

"That is rather efficient, don't you think?" Arthur declared as they both examined the photograph and caption below.

"Looks like we have our first three suspects right here, and a very good idea of where to find them."

"This is going to get expensive. I'd steak my life on it."

Chapter 4

Got a Chip on Your Shoulder?

UPON SEEING THE FRAMED NEWSPAPER CLIPPING AT Porter's Steak House, Arthur made a quick stop at a gas station before dropping Mackenzie off at her house. They both wanted a copy of the newspaper to read as the framed copy was just the photograph and caption. "See you Tuesday, bright and early," Arthur called to Mackenzie after she had already exited the vehicle and made it halfway to her front door.

"Not if I see you first." A grin crossed Mackenzie's face that she reserved only for Arthur.

Mackenzie plopped on her couch after losing the shoes and jacket at the door. "Where are my little hunters?" Two black flashes made their way to the living room. Before she could prepare herself fully, one 15-pound purr machine hopped in her lap and another, smaller version, started rubbing on her ankles. "What did you two get up to today?" Licorice and Caviar were two rescue cats that adopted Mackenzie shortly after she moved into the Birch Tree Lane house. They had run the house for about ten years now, and she didn't know how old they were when she brought them home. She appreciated every day they had together with a long session of chin scratches and belly rubs upon arriving home. She had just seen them before dinner, but that didn't matter.

The trio moved as one to the kitchen where she took out some raw food cat treats. It was really just cat food, but she gave it like treats, and they seemed to love it. "Well, we need to sit down and read this article. I'm struggling to figure out what my next move is." She returned to the couch with a blanket and the two snuggle bugs curled up between her legs. Now Mackenzie wished she had anticipated the inability to leave the couch. She would be thirsty soon and unable to move.

The article reported the details of the awards. No one looked happy in the photo except Bobby, and the final paragraph seemed to sum up the same conclusion. 'With temps roasting beyond medium, the fellow chefs did not seem overjoyed about the first-time winner.'

"Well, I guess I'd like to talk to these other chefs. Wonder if they'll still be broiling mad two days later." Mackenzie grabbed her phone to look up the three restaurants. As predicted, Well Dunn and Respect the Skirt were both closed on Mondays, but Nights in London Broil, the steakhouse owned and operated by Henry York, took off Tuesday nights instead. "Guess I'll be checking out British cuisine tomorrow. Who can I bring for a casual lunch that won't get suspicious if I'm asking a lot of questions?" She didn't want to bring

Arthur because he'd want to ask questions too. "I've got it. I'll bring Amy!"

Amy was the sweetest personal chef who occasionally helped Mac out if she had a large custom order or event. She wasn't cheap, but she was worth it. However, Amy was sometimes, well, a few yolks short of a soufflé when it came to life in general. Puns, jokes and anything that required making a conclusion based on subtlety went right over her head, but she could produce a four-course, Michelin-star quality dinner for twenty-five guests like she was a teenager playing a game of Tetris in the early nineties. She was good!

One phone call later and they had scheduled a lunch date for tomorrow at Nights in London Broil. Amy didn't ask any questions at all, just accepted the invite. Why would she ask any questions? Very few people knew Mackenzie was the one who found Bobby. Even after the Sunday paper missed out on the big story due to printing deadlines, WCSH had covered the story of Bobby's death on Sunday. She turned on the evening news because she could reach the remote without disturbing the sleeping princesses.

They were replaying the material from earlier in the day because the reporter on Dogwood Beach was clearly there in the morning or mid-day. They reported that there were few details to share at this time and would update the public if there was any known danger. Currently, they were treating this as an isolated homicide unless evidence came to light to support any other theories.

Mackenzie was relieved the details of her finding the body and the process of alerting the medical professionals and police were left out. She didn't want people asking her hundreds of questions or pitying her. She wanted to go out to lunch with Amy, enjoyable in and of itself, and see if she could dig up any important information in the process.

Her schedule as a bakery owner meant she slept odd hours. She had to go to bed early in order to be in the bakery for 3:30am, so on Mondays the cats were always confused. They would climb on her bed, and on her, make biscuits on the comforter and meow until she got up and fed them, regardless of when they had been fed last or if they were actually hungry; this meant she was often up much earlier than necessary on Monday mornings. She went for a walk – there were no runs in Mackenzie's schedule. She liked to say that if she was running, someone or something must be chasing her. The walk along the ocean was beautiful, even before sunrise. Today, though, she carried pepper spray, which she had never done before. With a killer on the loose, she wanted to make sure she was prepared.

After several weekly chores were checked off the list and plenty of time was spent with Licorice and Caviar, Mackenzie got ready for lunch. Nights in London Broil was close enough to walk to, but if she wanted to do anything after lunch, she'd need her car, so she drove to the steakhouse that was just on the other side of Dogwood.

The town of Dogwood was full of hustle and bustle

during the tourist months. There were dozens of shops selling every tchotchke imaginable with the name Dogwood or the image of the Dogwood flower front and center. Several ice cream shops that were dormant from October to April suddenly sprang to life in May. The steakhouses were some of the only restaurants that could stay open year round because of the Mainers who wanted food that felt home cooked.

Amy was waiting for Mackenzie in the parking lot. They hadn't seen much of each other lately, so this felt like a natural amount of time to catch up. Amy, of course, suspected nothing. Her 'Rachel' hairstyle had not changed since Jennifer Aniston made it famous on Friends, and it fit her perfectly. "Hey, Mac. Thanks for setting this up. Haven't seen you in ages." The two shared a brief embrace.

"I know. Felt the same, so here we are." The two women entered Nights in London Broil and looked around at an empty front of the house. No customers. No waitstaff. No hostess.

"Should we seat ourselves or check the kitchen for some staff?" Before they could peak into the kitchen, a flustered Chef York made his way to the front.

"Oh. Good afternoon. Didn't hear you come in. Alyssa! There are customers!" A woman, presumably Alyssa, hustled to the podium while Henry disappeared back into the kitchen.

"Good Afternoon. Sorry to keep you waiting. Please, follow me this way." As they strode through the dining room, she offered a four-top by the window or a two-top along the wall.

"This is fine." Mackenzie signaled to the table along the wall. "Wouldn't want to take up a larger table in case it gets busy." She understood the restaurant business but was also being sarcastic. As far as she knew, there were only four people in the whole building, including the three currently standing together.

The two friends sat and accepted the menus offered by Alyssa. "I will be back with you shortly."

Once Alyssa was out of earshot, Amy commented that she had never seen a restaurant actually empty before.

"Well, most restaurants aren't open on Mondays because it's statistically the slowest day of the week. That's why I'm closed today."

"Makes sense." Amy turned her attention to the menu. "This doesn't, though." Who pays for potato when you order a steak?"

"Henry modeled this place after high-end gastropubs in England. It's different, and people aren't taking to it as quickly as he would like. I've heard really great things about his food, but people around here expect things a certain way. Even though the final bill is similar, Mainers feel like it's a better deal to pay one price and have it include your starch and veg."

"Well, if Chef York wants to stay open, he might want to think about that."

Alyssa was on her way back to take drink and appetizer orders when they heard the Chef yell in the kitchen.

All three women ran to see what had happened, and a chorus of voices shouted questions.

"Is everything okay?"

"What happened?"

"Are you hurt?"

Chef York looked angry then immediately embarrassed. "Oh, I'm sorry. I forgot anyone was in here. There was an online article that made it seem like I was a suspect in Bobby's death. Why would anyone think that?" He walked over, phone in hand, to show them what he had been reading. The headline read, *Which Loser Stood to Lose the Most?* "With Bobby winning, he stood to get a lot of notoriety and business which would turn into profits. They are saying that I would lose money because I lost the contest. I mean, I was really hoping to win, but with the judges being locals who all knew Bobby, I wasn't holding out a lot of hope."

"The judges knew whose food they were voting for? That's not typical." Mackenzie made mental notes of all the things they needed to bring back to Arthur tomorrow morning.

"Yes, and they knew which places came with a cash prize. Bobby got $10,000 by winning. I didn't get any cash at all for coming in third runner-up, just some stupid participation trophy." He pointed to the small award on the shelf behind the line. "After leaving the awards, I came back here, put that bloody thing on the shelf and cooked myself a pity dinner."

"But what would make you think the article was accusing you of murder. It's not like you'd be upgraded to winner with Bobby dead?" Mackenzie was shocked Amy made such an obvious connection, but it was a good question.

"They're suggesting that by merely moving up the ladder to second runner-up, I'd get some money and my name would be listed in the Maine Restaurant Guide for the year. Third runner-up doesn't get on the list. Phone number, address, website...all of it would be added for Nights in London Broil by me moving up just one spot. That publication is a gold mine for restaurants all over the state."

"That's funny," observed Mackenzie. Based on the reactions of the other three in the room, the look of shock on her own face revealed that she didn't mean to say it out loud.

"What's funny?" Henry did not look like anything about this was funny. He was a proper British gentleman who stood straight and did not like to show too much emotion, especially not humor.

"Well, since Bobby's restaurant will probably still stay on the list in first place, even with him dead, you'd be more likely to be a suspect for murdering a judge out of anger than murdering Bobby."

"How will it stay open?" Henry scoffed and parts of his face went a bright shade of red, much like a person with rosacea.

"Oh, I had dinner there last night. The hostess said they are going to run it to keep the bills and staff paid until his family decides what to do.

The kitchen was silent.

"If you ladies will please return to your table, Alyssa will be happy to come take your order."

Alyssa escorted them back to their table and started by taking the drink and appetizer orders she initially came for before they were interrupted.

"So, that's one Moxie and one Coke, one escargot and one Caesar salad, no anchovies. I'll put that in and return in a few to take your entrée order."

"Moxie. Who even drinks Moxie anymore?"

"Grammy B loved it. I always think of her when I drink it. It's not often, but I feel close to her when I do."

"So, he was pretty upset about that article. Do you think he did it?" Amy arranged the cloth napkin on her lap.

"Not sure. Anger like that must come from somewhere real. Was he angry about the accusation or angry that it was accurate?

Alyssa came back with the drinks.

"Excuse me, but we were just wondering if the chef usually gets upset like that?" Mackenzie tried to look cute and innocent, though she could have just looked confused.

"Never. I've never seen him shout and get upset like that, and I've worked here two years."

"Thanks."

"Did you know what you wanted to order for your entrée?"

Mackenzie ordered a petite filet mignon with a side of chips, as the Brits called them, while Amy ordered the vegetarian wild mushroom pappardelle pasta. Alyssa headed to the kitchen with their orders.

"Amy, when did you become a vegetarian?"

"It was my New Year's resolution to try it."

"Then why did you agree to come to a steakhouse for lunch?"

"Because you asked, and I wanted to see you." Her response was so simple and honest – because Mackenzie had asked.

"Well, next time you choose, okay?"

"Sure." Amy happily accepted the salad as it was placed in front of her, and Mackenzie practically drooled over the escargot with the little cubes of puffed pastry on top. They enjoyed each other's company and caught up on what was happening at the bakery and in Amy's personal life over the course of the meal. When they were both finished, they returned to the parking lot and embraced once more, vowing not to let it go so long between times like this one.

Chapter 5

Seasoned Veterans

MACKENZIE DECIDED NOT TO DO ANYTHING EXCITING after lunch. She took the car just in case, but it started to drizzle, and she just didn't have anything she needed to do. The bakery and her cats were pretty much the focus of her existence, so the afternoon would be spent with Licorice, Caviar and a good book. Her Kindle library was full of titles she hadn't read yet, and today she would check one off the list. She mentally assessed what she might need on the couch for the next few hours: cell phone, drinks, snacks, blanket and iPad. The next decision was what to read. She still hadn't read *His Christmas List* by T L Swan, nor had she started the last SR Jones book, both in the romance genre but nothing alike. She decided, however, on this rainy Monday, to reread one of her favorites.

Agatha Christie books were another thing that made her feel close to Grammy B. There were stacks of mysteries all over this house when she lived here, and conversations over a cup of coffee usually included favorite red herrings and the best plot twists. Mackenzie must have read *And Then There Were None* a dozen times and seen every version that had ever been put on film. She would camp out with the future victims on an island and enjoy the classic whodunnit with the cats, happily recharging from her enlightening lunch with Amy.

Snuggled up on the love seat with a hot chocolate on the coffee table, she called to Licorice and Caviar to join her. No one showed up, so she started reading. By the time everyone had reached the island, both cats had cuddled up with her, and when the first death had occurred there was a knock at her door. She thought long and hard about whether to ignore the knock, but she couldn't run a scenario where that knock wasn't important. No one would be out selling anything in this weather at this time of year, and who really came to visit without calling her cell first anyway? Arthur.

She pulled her legs from beneath the blanket, attempting to leave the two cats undisturbed. She covered the closest, Licorice, with part of the blanket to encourage her to stay, hoping that whatever prompted this knock on her day off would not take long.

Looking through the window on her way to the door, she spotted Arthur's Volvo in the driveway. She opened the door and motioned for her friend to enter.

"Don't want to bother you on your day off. I just wanted to see if you read today's article about Bobby's death." He hesitated on the doorstep.

"Arthur, please come in. I can share some news with you as well." He entered and promptly removed his shoes, shaking his wet jacket outside before hanging it on the coat rack. Mackenzie would never have thought to purchase a coat rack, but Grammy B did so she owned one.

"Mackenzie, this article pretty much accuses the three chefs at that award ceremony of all having motive. I can't believe it was substantiated by any law enforcement, but all three are accused of profiting from Bobby's death."

"Well, my friend Amy and I went to Nights in London Broil for lunch and heard the reaction when Chef York read that same article. He was very angry and thought it was accusing him of the murder as well. I wonder what the other two chefs are thinking."

"What did Chef York say about the accusation?" Arthur was literally on the edge of the seat.

"He very clearly spelled out his motive. If he had moved up to the second runner-up position, he would have earned money and a coveted spot in some restaurant magazine that's apparently a very profitable advertising tool. He got third runner-up, a trophy and his picture in the paper. I couldn't tell if he was confessing or angry about the loss of revenue. When I told him Porter's was staying open, he nearly combusted and sent us to our table."

"Interesting. Well, it reads like all three had at least financial motives and at the top of that list was Mark

Dunn. He came in as first runner-up. Had Bobby not competed, he would have won."

"But it's odd to murder someone *after* the competition, right?"

"Mackenzie, what prompted you to go to lunch at Nights in London Broil today?"

"I wanted to see if there was any information to be gained from talking to Chef York."

"That's exactly why we need to go to Well Dunn."

"But they are closed on Mondays."

"Ahhh, but there is a private event tonight. The VA is hosting a dinner to thank businesses in the area who donate their time and resources to supporting or hiring veterans. Guess who just got a last-minute invitation as an employer of an elderly veteran?"

"No way. You've got to be kidding."

"I called to request that you be recognized for hiring a veteran with no experience when he had no other place to turn for a job and a purpose." Arthur looked at Mackenzie with the most adorable puppy dog eyes like she had saved his life by hiring him. "This will put us at the event, at Well Dunn, with Mark Dunn in attendance. We should be able to find a time to ask him some questions or at least listen in to any conversations he might be having."

Mackenzie had to admit she was impressed. "Arthur, that is one of the most resourceful things you've ever come up with. I commend you. Now, what do we need to wear, and what time is the event?"

"I'll pick you up at six forty-five sharp. You'll need to wear an evening gown, and I'll wear my dress uniform."

"Evening gown? You think I own an evening gown?" Mackenzie started to go into full panic mode.

"No, I don't think you own an evening gown. Why would you? You practically live at the bakery and on your day off you're sitting on the couch with your cats, a book and hot chocolate. No judgement here, but I can't think of any reason for you to have worn an evening gown since we met. I called a bridal shop in town that is open for another few hours. The owner said she has several dresses in stock you can try on for the event."

"I'm not going to buy an evening gown in order to try to interrogate a possible murder suspect."

"Ah ha! She said you can rent the gown for the night and return it tomorrow. I already gave her my credit card for the rental. Problem solved. Now, please get yourself ready, and I'll be back at six forty-five." Arthur then stood, replaced his shoes and coat, and let himself out.

"Guess there's no arguing with him, is there Caviar?" The cat didn't answer, as expected, so Mackenzie did as she was told.

Mackenzie walked out of Something New a couple hours later with a dress bag draped over her arm. She carefully laid it across the back seat of her car, vowing not to ruin the dress. If there was anything wrong that dry cleaning couldn't fix, she was responsible for the full price of the garment. That wasn't happening.

She returned home with enough time to shower again and do a full face of makeup and her hair. When Arthur returned to pick her up, she was objectively stunning. She opened the door and his jaw nearly hit the doorstep as did hers. Mackenzie had never seen Arthur in any uniform, though she had seen pictures of him when he was still in the military. Arthur had never seen Mackenzie in anything dressier than the cap-sleeved number she wore last night to dinner.

The shimmery orchid dress hugged her curves in all the right places and complemented the waves of thick red hair that cascaded over just her left shoulder. The halter neckline made her feel comfortable that nothing was going to fall out, but the shoes were a different story – there was nothing comfortable about those. She didn't want to spend a fortune on an outfit she would wear once, so she dug through the back of her closet and found strappy black heels that may have been from college.

"Mackenzie, you are breathtaking. I'll never understand how you are still single. Would you do me the honor of accompanying me to the dinner?" He presented her with a wrist corsage in a clear plastic box. "When I was younger, this was the thing to do. If you don't want to wear it, we can leave it here."

"I'd be honored." He slid the corsage onto her wrist. She grabbed a shawl, and they were off.

When they entered Well Dunn, several other veterans were also in full uniform. Mackenzie was able to follow Ret. Lt. General Arthur Johnson around as he rubbed elbows. She didn't know much about military service other than a few stories she heard from an uncle and some cousins who had served. However, she did hear others mentioning the bronze star and distinguished service medals. Knowing those were very important, she made a mental note to ask Arthur more questions about those at a later date.

Remembering the reason they were at the dinner to begin with, Mackenzie tipped her head in the direction of the kitchen when she noticed Mark Dunn walking into the dining space. No one had taken seats yet, so she excused herself from the lively joint memories of KP duty and headed in Mark's direction.

"Good evening, Mr. Dunn. This is a lovely dinner you have organized for the veterans."

"Well, thank you. Really, though, it's for the employers who support the veterans. Have I seen you before?" Mark looked her down and back up. It gave Mackenzie an icky feeling the way he moved his eyes over her body.

"Mr. Dunn, I am here as the owner of Top O' the Muffin to Ya, the bakery in the center of Cozy Cove." Since Well Dunn was technically in Dogwood, it was possible but not probable that Mark had never driven into Cozy Cove. It was more probable that he had never been in the bakery. Mackenzie's hair, however, did stand out as unique, so that's probably – hopefully – what he remembered about her.

"Oh, right. I think I've been in there once or twice

with my wife." That look certainly didn't say husband material to Mackenzie. She took a deep breath to collect herself.

"I wanted to congratulate you on the recognition from the Grilling Association of Southern Maine. Quite the accomplishment." She watched his face, waiting to read the reaction. There was a flash of anger, maybe frustration, before a forced fake smile.

"Thank you. First runner-up is nothing to sneeze at."

"I'd be pretty broiled if I knew the judges were friendly with the winner." Now Mark couldn't hold in his true feelings.

"Yes, that did fry my Rocky Mountain oysters. Didn't know that ahead of time."

"Guess it didn't pay off as well as he hoped." She hoped she had hit the right snarky tone.

"What do you mean? Bobby got first place, ten grand and a better trophy." Mark pointed to his trophy on the mantle over the fireplace, the centerpiece of the dining room.

"Where do I start? I saw the photo in the newspaper. You all looked, if I may say, less than impressed with the winner. And let's not forget, he's dead."

"I'm not trying to be insensitive. I know he's dead."

"Was killed. The police are investigating a homicide." Mackenzie hoped Mark was angry enough to spill something. She looked over her shoulder briefly to check on Arthur who was still chatting away with the same group.

"I did know that, but his restaurant, from what I

heard, is staying open. Even in death, he's still competition."

"Does that rub you the wrong way?"

"Look, I'm not saying it wouldn't be nice to have less competition. Any businessman, or woman, would love to have less competition. And that location. Who wouldn't want a chance to have a larger seating capacity? That view alone would add two or three dollars onto each entrée." Mackenzie could write a small book with the number of motives Mark just confessed to. "Whatever the case, I feel badly for his family and employees."

"Did I also hear that there was some magazine or something that your name will be listed in because you were a top-three finisher?"

"Yea, but as long as you're listed, it's pretty great free advertising. I'm bummed I only won five grand, but I'm proud of the rest."

"Did you go out to celebrate after the awards?"

"Nah. Went home and watched Burnt. Felt appropriate."

Mackenzie noticed people were starting to take their seats.

"I didn't mean to keep you so long. I'll go take my seat. Thank you for putting this event on."

"Thank *you* for being an employer that supports veterans."

Mackenzie walked across the room to sit next to Arthur. He stood as she approached and pulled out her seat for her. "Learn anything?"

"Too much to say here and now." She smiled at the

rest of their tablemates and sat, accepting assistance from Arthur when he pushed in her chair.

The food was good, company better, and the cause was the best! The whole evening was to thank employers like Mackenzie, but the way she admired Arthur proved that she felt like having him in her life was the very best surprise that she had ever received. She did accept a framed certificate of recognition to hang in her bakery, but the real gift was Arthur's company. They drove back to her house together after a few hours of food, fun and laughter that she would surely regret when her alarm went off a three in the morning. The dress was still in great condition, so she wouldn't need to spend the extra money, though she did fall in love with it. Her feet, however, would pay the highest price for the night.

"Arthur, I'd love to go over everything about Mark, but I really need to get to sleep. Tomorrow will come too quickly. I do want to thank you, though."

"For what? Securing the invitation was no big deal."

"For the first time in a very long time, I felt appreciated. I felt attractive. I felt like more than just my bakery. Thank you for giving that to me tonight." Mackenzie gave Arthur a soft peck on the cheek before opening her own car door and walking up to the front of her house. She'd be seeing Arthur again very soon, if history was to repeat itself, and she'd have plenty of time in the kitchen to recall the events of the evening before customers showed up.

Chapter 6

Great Pastry Chefs Take Whisks

Mackenzie wished it was bright and early when she got to work – it was dark and early because the sun hadn't risen yet. As predicted, Arthur was already in the shop because he was given a key after about a year working alongside Mackenzie. He knew her routine so well, he already had lights and machines on, towels laid out at the appropriate stations and the register counted and ready to go. How he had so much energy at his age, she'd never know.

"How would you like your orange juice this morning, mug or glass?" Arthur thought he was being funny, but it was adorable. Regardless of the fact she owned and operated a business that focused on breakfast and snacks, she didn't drink coffee, espresso, tea or any other typical morning energy booster. Orange juice was her favorite, and freshly squeezed was the way to her heart. "I know you'd prefer I squeezed the oranges myself, but there were none in the fridge this morning."

"No oranges in the fridge? I need to make cranberry-orange muffin tops. Those always sell well Tuesday through Thursday when people pretend they are healthy."

"I know, and I already plan to make a run to the store as soon as it opens at six."

"What would I do without you?" Mackenzie took a deep breath, accepted her mug of orange juice, which was always the correct answer to the question Arthur asked, and strode confidently through to the kitchen.

She was a machine. The way Mackenzie multi-tasked was masterful. When one oven was baking muffins the other one was being unloaded of coffee cakes to cool so they could be frosted later. When both ovens were occupied, she made batter for the next sweet treat. Arthur watched in wonder until the drill sergeant emerged, demanding the location of an ingredient right in front of her face. She always apologized for the hours before the shop opened, and he always told her it was no problem. There was a break in the duo's action while Arthur sourced the missing oranges, but they were still ready to operate, right on time. As it was Tuesday, one of the specialty items in the case was a flourless chocolate torte, so she slipped on her *Life is Torte, Take Whisks* apron before opening the doors.

Arthur spent the next few hours thinking about everything Mackenzie had reviewed with him about her discussions with Mark Dunn and Henry York. If he heard correctly, it sounded like not only did Mark envy the size and location of Porter's, but he didn't have an alibi. After careful thought, he realized Henry York didn't have an alibi either, but he did have a motive of putting his British restaurant on the Maine map. If Bobby's restaurant closed as a result of his death, there would be no reason to have Porter's in the restaurant guide, leaving the third spot open for Nights in London Broil. This was getting juicy.

"Arthur. Arthur, can you please get two coffee cakes for Mrs. Jones, to go?"

"Sorry, Mac. Little distracted."

"Well, don't let it happen again. Might have to find someone else willing to work for free."

Arthur rolled his eyes. Since his first days, Mackenzie had been able to start paying him for more hours, but he only put on his timecard what he knew she could afford. He wasn't senile just yet. If it had been a slow week, he put in for his agreed-upon ten hours for Saturday and Sunday. On good weeks, he put in for fifteen or twenty.

The shift went smoothly with slower moments in between the occasional mad dashes. Both Mackenzie and Arthur were watching the clock to see when they both felt it safe to close up, even if it was before 2pm, when the person walking through the door gave them each a newly found burst of energy. Brandy Kelly was the last chef pictured in the newspaper article alongside the murdered Bobby Porter, and neither Arthur nor Mackenzie had spoken with her yet. The only problem was, what would they say? Neither had come up with a plausible motive for Brandy.

"Good afternoon. How can we help you?"

"I am in a terrible rush to get back to my restaurant, but I need to pick up pastries and goodies for my staff."

"Oh, are you celebrating something?" Mackenzie saw an opening and took it.

"Well, in case you didn't hear, I was the second runner-up in the Grillers of Southern Maine contest for Griller of the Year. It's a big deal to get in the restaurant guide, and I just snuck in!"

Mackenzie and Arthur gave each other a look. Second runner-up was an odd thing to be celebrating.

"Congratulations are in order. What would you like from the case?" Arthur began assembling a to-go box large enough for several pastries. "Everything was baked fresh this morning."

"Oh, just put in one or two of everything until you get to, say, twenty-five pieces."

"Can do." Arthur loaded all of the most expensive pieces first, two at a time, to help with the register for the day.

"I did see that newspaper article," recalled Mackenzie. "The only chef that looked happy was Bobby. The rest of you looked like you could kill him."

"From what I heard, someone succeeded."

Mackenzie couldn't believe what she was hearing. "Excuse me?"

"I heard that Bobby Porter was stabbed to death. Some couple found him on Dogwood Beach with a hole in his gut." Not only did Brandy sound happy about Bobby's death, but it could also be mistaken for bragging if she knew what Mackenzie knew.

"I found Bobby's body." Makenzie spoke the words, and Arthur whipped his head around.

All of the color drained from Brandy's face. "You what?"

"I was half of the couple that found Bobby's body on the beach. It was awful."

Brandy was speechless. She looked to Arthur to save her as her eyes gave away the rewind presently happening in her memory, wondering how much she had just said.

"So," Mackenzie started, "what else do you know about Bobby's murder? I've been thinking about it non-stop since Saturday night and if you have any other information to share, I'd love to hear it."

"Ummm...no. I don't. Everything I said was just rumors and gossip. I feel so bad now that I've repeated it. Was anything untrue?"

Mackenzie thought for a moment about lying and telling Brandy a false story just to see if she spread it to the greater community, but she decided against it for Bobby's sake. "While vague, nothing was untrue. Maybe just think about who you are speaking with when it involves a death."

Arthur finished packaging up the pastries for Brandy to take to her staff. He handed them to Mackenzie who slid them across the counter. "Here you go," she said, happily. "On the house."

"Oh no, I couldn't possibly take them without paying."

"Just an area business supporting another area business. We're very happy for you and your team to be recognized. Anything that brings business to the area is good for all of us."

Brandy looked skeptical but accepted the boxes.

"Thank you. I'll let the staff know about your generosity." As she turned to walk away, she said, "Have a nice day."

The door closed behind her strutting backside.

"I wish I could strangle her with those braids."

"You better watch out, Mac, or people will start thinking you're a suspect."

"I know there is absolutely no physical evidence to support her being the murderer, but I just have a gut feeling she was responsible or involved."

"It was pretty easy to read how you felt about her. I was shocked you gave her all of that product for free. She would have gladly paid you."

"I'll write it off as a donation."

"That's the Mackenzie I know."

"Let's close up now. We don't have much left and there's no reason for me to make anything else at this point in the day. I think I want to go for a walk."

"You're the boss, boss."

They cleaned up the shop in silence. Other than the cars that passed by the shop to go further into Cozy Cove, there was only the occasional scraping of the chairs on the tiled floor as Arthur prepared the dining area for tomorrow's customers. The cases were clean, the appliances in the kitchen spotless, and the fridges were full of ingredients just waiting for Mackenzie to turn them into something amazing.

"Well, we've done all we can do for today. Have a great afternoon."

"You too, Mac." Without turning around, he shouted, "Hey, life is what you bake it." As if it was his mic drop moment, Arthur left the shop first, making his way to the reliable old Volvo. There was one reserved parking spot on the bakery property, and Mackenzie didn't use it. She walked over the bridge to get to work each morning and assigned the coveted spot to Arthur years ago. Today was no exception. After locking up, Mackenzie turned left to walk along the exposed side of the bakery where a one-way road took up every available inch of space, not even leaving enough room for a sidewalk. If you wanted to get somewhere in Cozy Cove, you walked in the street along with the cars.

Without a destination in mind, Mackenzie sauntered west, further along the peninsula. She walked by several shops selling t-shirts and sweatshirts, depending on the weather, and two different take-out windows with signage promising the best lobster roll in Maine. She smiled as she walked by the familiar chalkboard menus on the half-doors that served as security at night and advertising space during the day. One shop had a traditional cold lobster roll with mayonnaise, celery and a toasted bun. In the summer, she often watched the employees carry the crustaceans directly from the boats to the counter when a steamed lobster was ordered. Today, though, there was just one person at the counter working on a crossword puzzle and no customers. Two storefronts down boasted an award-winning hot lobster roll. Whether you poured the hot melted butter on or mixed the lobster meat in the butter and lemon before placing it in the bun, this oceanic treat was often called a Connecticut lobster roll – just don't tell the owners that. Due to the chill in the air, a line formed at this window, even though it was past the lunch hour.

Between the two lobster shacks was a photographer's shop. Though she had never purchased any pieces from the artist, Mackenzie often browsed through the store-front windows. Today, she thought, was the day she would buy something. Adjust Your Focus was a very narrow shop that went back for a distance, allowing for many pieces to be shown on the side walls. Rotating stands along the middle of the floor showcased postcards and customizable ornaments for sale. She assumed the postcards were photographs taken by the artist, but the ornaments looked more like something that had been brought in to attract the eye of tourists passing by. "Hel-lo?" Mackenzie called back to see if there was anyone working.

"Coming!" shouted a happy voice from behind what she assumed to be an office door. "Good afternoon. My name is Brian. How can I help you?" Pale blue eyes met hers, and the half-smile on the man's face revealed a single dimple in his right cheek.

"I was just admiring your ornaments. Did you make them?"

"No. As a matter of fact, they were made by my

niece. She allows me to put them in my shop, and I pay her when they sell. I'd be happy to add a date or names on them if you'd like."

"I haven't decided what I want yet, but I'll let you know. I was also admiring the postcards. These seem to be in the same style as your work on the walls. Do you have ones for various businesses in the area?"

"I'm not sure I understand what you mean."

"I was wondering if you had considered photographing local businesses and selling your postcards to them to resell in their shops. If you wanted to photograph my bakery cases, for example, you could sell postcards here but also sell some to me where I could feature them in my bakery and also direct people to your shop, and vice versa back to mine."

"What a great idea! I never thought of something like that before. Could I start with yours, tomorrow maybe?"

Mackenzie's hand rose to her hairline in a thoughtful gesture when she realized what she must look like after a full day of working and getting up before dawn. There was nothing she could do about it, so being the confident woman she was, she pressed on. "I'd love that. If you want to come before we open to the public, I'll make sure to have the cases full with lots of bright colors and some fancy pieces. What do you think?"

"It's a great idea to support each other like that. What time can I arrive?"

"Let's start with 6:30am, that way you'll have at least thirty minutes, and I can move things around if you need me to for the best shots. I was thinking, I'm sure most businesses would welcome the free publicity in Cozy Cove and Dogwood. My bakery shows up on your post-card rack, reminding people to come get a yummy treat, and your postcards sit on my counter with a sign reminding people to visit your shop...it's a win-win for any business, including yours."

"I can't believe we found each other today. What did you say your name was?" The gentleman lifted his strong but gentle hand to shake Mackenzie's. She watched their hands touch, causing the hairs on her arms to stand up as if there were static electricity in the air. He stood several inches taller than she did, so when she looked up to meet his eyes again, his half smile turned into a full smile, revealing a second dimple.

"Mackenzie, but most people call me Mac."

"Well, Mackenzie, I'll see you tomorrow morning at 6:30am sharp."

The way he said her name made something in her tummy flutter. She would not go so far as to call them butterflies because she wasn't in her twenties anymore, but it was something similar to butterflies. "Yes, I'll see you then." She turned to leave the shop and realized she hadn't purchased anything. "Oh, I forgot to pick out an ornament."

"Don't worry about it. We'll get together to pick the photos for your postcards and you can choose one then, since it guarantees I'll get to see you again." There were those butterfly-like feelings again.

"Sounds good. Tomorrow."

She walked out of the shop and continued again

toward the back of the land mass that projected out into the ocean. Mackenzie's walk was different now. She wondered how she had never met this tall and dimpled newcomer before. She knew there was an artist's shop there for years, but not too long ago the windows in the front lost their pottery and stone pieces, replaced by paintings and framed photography. In the months since the switch, she hadn't been in.

Her feet carried her all the way back to the rocky area where the ocean waves crashed at high tide. Next to her, as if calling to her, stood Porter's Steak House. She had just eaten here on Sunday and not two days later, she stood here, feeling like there were more answers inside. A late lunch alone didn't really excite her, but she wanted to know what those answers were. She decided that she could eat a small lunch before getting back to her precious fur babies that were probably very lonely at this time of day. One foot in front of the other, she entered the restaurant.

Chapter 7

Who's the Rarest of Them All

"Back so soon?" The tall blonde from Sunday was at the podium again.

"I'm sorry, I didn't catch your name last time."

"Heidi. I'm the manager for the front of the house. I presume everything was to your liking last time."

"Well, Heidi, it was a wonderful meal. My compliments to the chef. Just looking for a light lunch today. I run the bakery..."

"Top O' the Muffin to Ya. Yes! I knew I'd seen you before Sunday. My friends and I get breakfast from you most weekends. Everyone takes turns picking up, so I've only been in a couple times recently. I remembered your hair when you were in before." It wasn't a compliment worthy of a thank you, so the two women looked at each other awkwardly.

It seemed everyone remembered Mackenzie's hair. There was nothing bad about it now that she was a secure adult, but the teasing for being a ginger wasn't easy growing up. The only irritating part now was being asked for the shade of dye she used, though dye had never touched a single hair on her head. And why would anyone, with the perfect shade of copper her family lineage had blessed her with.

"Any chance you have a small table near the window?"

"We're slow now, and I have a two-top available. Right this way."

Mackenzie remembered that she wanted to write up a review, so she planned to do just that on her phone once she ordered. While she strongly believed it was rude to be on your phone while out to dinner with someone, solo diners seemed to get a pass in her book of etiquette.

"Here you are." Heidi handed her a menu and gestured to the small, round table. "The specials today are a well-done porterhouse, London broil and a petite skillet-seared skirt steak."

"Any chance that's a dig at the competition?" Mackenzie couldn't help but notice the names of the other chefs' restaurants in the specials. Mark Dunn would be furious to be mentioned in the same special as the T-shaped cut from the rear end of the short loin. Henry York was so oblivious about naming his restaurant after a meal first cooked in Philadelphia, he probably wouldn't notice or care. It was very clear by the time the last special was named that Brandy Kelly would put it together as a dig at her restaurant, likening the meal to a miniskirt. Mackenzie thought it was all quite funny.

"I'd have to ask the chef. Jason created the specials for today."

"Interesting. I thought I heard that things hadn't changed here in three generations, then not even when Bobby took over. Steak and potatoes had always worked, so why change it if it ain't broke, right?"

Heidi blushed and didn't quite know what to say. "Um, I'd be happy to let the chef know you have questions for him. If he gets a chance, I'm sure he'll come out to your table."

"If he has time, I'd love to speak with him." Mackenzie began to inspect the menu, so Heidi backed up then turned around and left for the kitchen. She didn't see a waitress at any tables for at least five minutes. When one eventually came, she was frazzled.

"How are you enjoying your meal?"

"I haven't ordered yet. Is everything alright?"

The waitress looked down at the empty table. "I'm so sorry. I'm the only server on today, so it's been hectic."

Mackenzie scanned the dining room. There were only a few tables with customers, and they were all already eating. She couldn't figure out how this waitress could be so overworked. "Well, I'm all set to order if that would be possible."

"Absolutely. What can I get you?"

"I'd like to order the steak pot pie. Can I get a loaded baked potato as well, please?" If she hadn't just worked a ten-hour shift serving food she couldn't eat, she might feel guilty. When it came to food, Mackenzie owned every calorie with pride.

"Sure thing. Anything to drink?"

"Do you have real iced tea or the fake kind that's sweetened?

"The fake kind," the waitress said, apologetically, "but we have sweetened and unsweetened."

"Perfect. Sweetened please with a slice of lemon. Thanks." Mackenzie handed the menu over to the waitress, and she walked to the computer to enter the order.

It was brighter in the restaurant this time, so Mackenzie really took a look at the décor. The tables and chairs looked like they had been there since Bobby's great-grandfather opened the restaurant. The wood paneling screamed 1970s and the carpet, well, it needed to be replaced. The only part of the restaurant that looked updated was the glass wall facing the ocean. The steaks were good and service had always been acceptable, but people came here for the view. Other restaurants in Cozy Cove with a view of the ocean were more like a quick service where you carried your own food to a table with a plastic cover. Porter's was considered fine dining, though Mackenzie was starting to change her mind after having recently dined at two of the competitors. She could see now why Mark was so disappointed that Porter's was staying open. If she owned a steakhouse, she'd want this address as well.

The waitress checked on the other tables after entering Mackenzie's order and disappeared into the kitchen. Returning with the lemon and iced tea, she looked much more composed. "Here you go."

"Excuse me." For the first time, Mackenzie eyed the

name tag on the waitress's shirt. Her name was Paula. That seemed to Mackenzie like a name for someone much older. This Paula looked like she was in her early twenties. "I was just wondering if you have worked here long?"

"Over two years, I think. Why?"

"Well, first, please accept my condolences at losing Bobby. I'm sure he is missed." Paula's face was neutral, and Mackenzie didn't know what message that was sending. "I was just wondering if things have changed recently, since his passing."

"Well, if you mean Jason telling us we're running a brand-new menu starting next Tuesday, I'd say things are changing. I have to come in Monday, my day off, to try everything and learn the menu so I can keep my job." The look on Paula's face spoke volumes. First, she showed her true feelings of anger and resentment across her whole face, then, presumably when she realized what she'd said to a customer, her eyes showed shock and regret. "Oh, I shouldn't have said that. I'm so sorry to complain to you."

"No, I totally get it. I'd feel the same way. Did he say why he's changing the menu?"

"He didn't. Just said things around here were changing for the better and he hoped everyone was ready to get on board."

Mackenzie noticed a table waiting to leave. She motioned to Paula to look in their direction. "Sorry to keep you."

"That's fine. Sorry to unload on you." She turned and headed to the other table.

Mackenzie learned a lot about the true feelings surrounding Bobby by just sitting back and listening to those who knew him. When she realized she still hadn't written that review, she took out her phone. She snapped a photo of the view from her table so she could post it with her review. A plate of piping hot food was placed on her table, just as she logged in to start typing. Above her stood the chef. She knew this because she read his name, Chef Bell, embroidered on the front of his white jacket.

"I heard you wanted to ask a few questions."

Jason was younger than she expected. It wasn't often the head chef of an award-winning restaurant looked to be in his mid-twenties. "Yes. The specials today...were they meant to be a dig at Bobby's competitors in the grilling competition?"

Jason chuckled. "I wondered if anyone would pick up on that. I intended it as an inside joke but knew there was a possibility someone would get it. Good job...I'm sorry, what's your name?"

"Mackenzie Walsh. I own Top O' the Muffin to Ya."

"Never been."

"You have to drive by it to get here. The yellow building with the double doors, big sign above the door with a muffin on it."

"I'll have to take a look for it tomorrow. Well, I'll let you enjoy your meal."

"Actually, I heard a rumor there were big changes coming. Did Bobby's family decide to go in a different direction after all these years?" Mackenzie knew she was fishing and nothing might come of it, but she had to try.

"The family gave me free license to do what I felt was best for the restaurant and staff to keep the bills paid. I've worked under Bobby for a year now, and it's time for a change."

"To be trusted with a restaurant like Porter's, you must have experience prior to working under Bobby. Were you a sous chef somewhere else first?" She could see there was a fire building behind his eyes. Jason did not seem to want to continue answering questions, but he looked like a rodent caught in a trap, almost willing to gnaw off his own limb.

"I worked under Brandy Kelly for a while before here. Was there anything else you needed?"

"Last question, I promise. What made you leave one steakhouse for another? From the customer point of view, they don't seem that much different."

"Let's just say there was more room for growth under Bobby. Brandy wasn't exactly worried about my success. I was a good little worker who helped put her on the map. When I interviewed with Bobby, I felt like I was going to be part of a team. That meant a lot to me."

"I'd love to see Bobby's trophy from Saturday night. Is it displayed somewhere?" Both Mackenzie and Jason searched the perimeter of the dining room.

"I'm not sure where it ended up. I'll ask his family because we'd love to have it here on display."

"Well, thanks for humoring me. It was nice getting to know you. I can't wait to dig into my pie and potato."

"Have a nice meal. I'll try to stop by your bakery sometime." With that empty promise, he returned to the kitchen.

Mackenzie was shocked she couldn't locate the actual trophy, but she was sure that wasn't the top priority for anyone in the family right now. The revelation that Jason had once worked for Brandy was new. She'd have to file that in the 'remember to tell Arthur' drawer of her mental filing cabinet. She knew that finding a reason to talk to Brandy was even more important now. Having worked with Jason had nothing to do with motive or an alibi, but Mackenzie still felt uneasy after the interaction this afternoon.

When she had eaten every last morsel on her plate and left a glowing review of the steak pot pie online, she waved to Paula who now only had just the one active table, Mackenzie's.

"How was everything? I saw you got to chat with Chef Bell."

"The chef was nice. Sounds like you are in for some changes. I promise I did not mention you. I wish you the best of luck under his direction." Mackenzie hoped she sounded convincingly sincere.

"Thanks. It's a good job, especially in the summer."

Mackenzie handed over her credit card, which she typically tried not to use, and finished her iced tea. When Paula returned with the card and receipt to sign, she thanked Mackenzie again and walked away. The lunch was pleasant and service informative, so she left a good tip. When she got to the front door to leave, she examined the framed newspaper photograph again. Yes, all four chefs had a trophy in their hands. It still seemed odd that Bobby's wasn't here. Where else would it be? Actually, he probably never made it back to the restaurant between the awards and his death, so somewhere in between made the most sense. It didn't really matter, so she exited the establishment and walked the rest of the way around the one-way loop, back to the front of her business. She checked, just to be sure, that the signage was still above the front of the shop. Everything was as it should be, blueberry muffin and all.

The cove was pretty quiet today, and Mackenzie had no plans for what was left of the daylight. She decided to continue the walk a little longer and follow the path that stayed parallel to the shoreline for about a mile. The return trip started to get a little cool, and she still had to walk the rest of the way home after taking the bridge on the northern side of the cove.

During the walk, Mackenzie thought about how Jason had worked for Brandy and now was in charge of Porter's. Did he tell her the truth? Did he leave Respect the Skirt for professional advancement or something else? Based on his current trajectory at Porter's, he wasn't shy about taking risks and causing waves. Was it possible he caused too many waves at his former position that he was actually fired? As the saying goes, there's two halves to every bagel. Mackenzie had to find a reason to visit Brandy and see if she had a rebuttal without knowing she had one. What excuse could there possibly be to show up to yet another steakhouse and grill the owner?

When Mackenzie reached her front door, she was greeted by her two fur babies. She gave them plenty of attention while she recapped the day. When she got to the part about meeting Brian, her tone changed. "He was very polite, you know. His hand was firm but gentle at the same time. Oh dear, I totally forgot he's coming to the shop tomorrow. I need to let Arthur know and get some sleep to prepare for the photo's he's taking." And with that, Mackenzie called Arthur to let him know the plan. She made sure Licorice and Caviar had plenty of food and water, and Mackenzie crawled into bed earlier than she could ever remember. She didn't fall asleep immediately, but when she did, she had an image of Brian in her head and a smile on her lips.

Chapter 8

This is How We Roll

THE ALARM CLOCK WENT OFF AT 3AM WITH Mackenzie already in the shower. She could feel that today was going to be a day of great things; what those things were remained a mystery to her. She was walking across the bridge on the way to work with a skip in her step she hadn't felt in a long time. Brian would be getting there in a few short hours, and her bakery case needed to look better than ever before. In the shower, she figured out how she was going to kill two birds with one stone herself. All of the amazing treats she needed to create would never sell on a Wednesday. She would spend more money on product than she could ever make back for a weekday morning. She decided to risk it all by making everything for the photo shoot before contacting Brandy.

The plan Mackenzie devised while showering was to bring an assortment of desserts that Brandy could offer at Respect the Skirt. She could make the number and type of desserts to order each afternoon when things started to get slow and Brandy, or an assistant, could pick them up each day for that evening's patrons to order from. This partnership would also allow people to order specialty celebration desserts with a 24-hour notice. While this was a great business decision for the bakery, it also allowed Mackenzie the opportunity to get some one-on-one time with Brandy this afternoon, as long as she agreed to the last-minute meeting.

Arthur showed up earlier than usual to help with both plans. He assisted in the kitchen more than ever, frosting things that didn't require too much artistic talent. The mini-Bundt cakes had a generous amount of white sugary goodness coating every surface, and the spritz cookies shone with decorative sugar on top. These were not typically offered outside the month of December, but they would look good for the postcards. She also snuck in a blueberry pie and whoopie pies for the bottom of the case.

At 6:27am, a hand pressed against the glass of the front door to the bakery. Brian, shielding his eyes, attempted to spot Mackenzie but got Arthur instead. Arthur opened the door and cautiously welcomed Brian inside. Attempting to make himself as tall as possible, Arthur stretched his back and neck as long and straight as he could. Brian had a calm persona, happy to answer the multitude of questions thrown at him. A casual observer would liken this interaction to a dad grilling his daughter's date on prom night.

"Just out of high school, I served two four-year tours with the U.S. Army around the middle east in the late 1990s and early 2000s. After that, I was training new recruits at different bases in the states. I retired from the military after twenty years of service and have lived in Maine ever since. I always loved photography and figured it might make a good hobby and business for the rest of my working years."

Arthur nodded at Brian's history with his pointer finger and thumb holding his chin. Before he could respond, Mackenzie burst through the swinging doors into the shop front.

"Where is he? I can't believe...oh, hi, Brian." Mackenzie had her hair up off the nape of her neck in a low bun while escaped tendrils framed her face.

"Good morning. He is right here, on time. Let me know when you are ready for me, and I can get out of here as quickly as possible."

"Oh, you don't need to get out quickly, but we open at 7am, so there might be people in your way."

"Well, let's get cooking."

Arthur felt it was his duty to correct Brian's attempt at a pun. "This is a bakery. A better option would be, let's bake the world a better place." Mackenzie rolled her eyes, and Brian chuckled.

"Let's bake the world a better place." Brian smirked and took his camera out to get started.

"I have a few more things to get ready for the day. Please feel free to holler back if you need me to move anything or change anything in the case."

"Mackenzie, I can help Brian. Do whatever it is you need to get done to be ready to open on time. We've got this."

She smiled and returned to the kitchen. When she came out to open the shop, Brian was gone.

"Where did he go?" Mackenzie's face fell.

"He said he didn't want to bother you since it was getting so close to opening and that he would bring you some pictures to choose from tomorrow. I think I like him." Arthur stepped behind the counter and tied on his waist apron, ready for the day.

Mackenzie unlocked the door, flipped the closed sign to open and added her statement apron to the front of her outfit. Above a smiling cartoon cinnamon roll read, They See Me Rollin'.

Several hours and dozens of customers later, an uncharacteristically busy Wednesday started to wrap up. Mackenzie called Respect the Skirt around eleven to set up an afternoon meeting with Brandy. She offered to bring a sample of potential desserts for her to try, and they would run some numbers regarding costs and possible profits for the restaurant. When it got to a point where Arthur could keep up, Mackenzie went back into the kitchen to create a few custom items, including a gluten-free brownie and a sugar-free layered pudding with a pecan crust. This was going to look as authentic as possible while still being a covert investigation.

Arthur offered to close the front of the shop and lock up so Mackenzie could head out a little early for the meeting. Since the kitchen was already clean, he was really offering to wash the floors and wipe any glass that needed wiping. She thanked him profusely for offering his car as well. She needed to transport all of the desserts and would be late if she walked back to her house first to get her car. Arthur would walk to Mackenzie's house and wait for her to get back from the meeting – he had a key for that too.

She pulled the Volvo into a spot near the rear entrance to Respect the Skirt and started removing boxes of desserts. As she got to the door, Brandy was there to open it for her. "Right on time. Need any help?"

"Nah. It'll just take me one more trip to get the other boxes." She struggled to balance everything but made it to an empty counter successfully. "I'll be right back." Mackenzie returned with the remainder of the desserts and repeated the struggle to not drop anything. Brandy had servers carry everything to a private dining area adjacent to the kitchen so they could try the desserts.

Brandy, her sous chef Angela and the hostess sat around the table with glasses of water to sample the products Mackenzie had painstakingly crafted. Mackenzie did her best to hide the look of disappointment on her face due to the presence of the additional taste testers. Getting Brandy alone was part of the plan.

Mackenzie started with slices of blueberry pie. Being the state dessert of Maine, it's a must-have for any respectable restaurant. The crust was perfect and flaky.

Soggy bottom crusts were simply not allowed. It wasn't going to be popular, necessarily, but she served whoopie pies second. Even though it was the official state treat of Maine, the origin was a bit muddled as several states claim to have invented them. All three women around the table spoke highly of the treat, but no one wanted it on the dessert menu. Third was a decadent chocolate layer cake with thick chocolate frosting. Everyone agreed this was going to be the number one dessert, regardless of what else came out of those boxes. However, as Mackenzie was opening the box with the gluten-free brownies, the hostess, Mandy, said, "Remember when Jason was working here and got you a chocolate cake for your birthday?" She pointed in Brandy's direction. "He was so proud of himself until you told him you didn't see things working out between you two, so he quit."

There it was. Mackenzie had an opening to ask the question she wanted to ask, hoping to cause a reaction from someone at the table. "So, Jason quit because of the cake and not to take the job at Porter's?" The three women stared. Mackenzie wasn't part of the group, and, according to the glares coming from the three tasters sitting at the table, her question was received as very inappropriate. She needed to figure out a way to get on the same wavelength as them. "I mean, I was just at Porter's and he was bragging how he left here to make a big career move with Bobby." If she put Jason down, who did not seem to be in favor with these women, they may accept her as being on their side.

"Oh, he said that did he? Not true. He was all hurt that I wouldn't date him."

"He followed Brandy around like a little puppy dog the whole time he worked here and was crushed when she shot him down," Angela chimed in.

"We got the impression he was trying to get back at Brandy by taking the job with Bobby and starting to date the front of the house manager in the same week." Mandy looked to Brandy, checking if she had said too much. From the sad look on Brandy's face, she had.

"Oh, I'm so sorry, Brandy. That's awful. And now, he and Heidi are running the place together. Big changes coming, I heard." This was another subtle attempt by Mackenzie to join the group, and it was working. The brownies were plated and served with a scoop of vanilla ice cream that she had carried with her in a small cooler. "The gluten-free brownie serves two purposes. It gives people who require gluten-free foods the ability to get dessert, and you have a good dessert choice for children at a full-size price. Servers can suggest it when you have young diners. All three of the desserts you seem to like so far can be served with vanilla ice cream, which means you only have to stock that one flavor."

Brandy brought the conversation back to Porter's. "What big changes are you hearing about at Porter's?"

Mackenzie had her just where she wanted her. "Jason has full control of the menu and is training staff for the menu changes next week."

"And Heidi is still at the front of the house?"

"Sure is. She sat me for a late lunch yesterday. I didn't see any interaction between them, though."

By the tension in her fists, Brandy looked fired up, but Mackenzie was intent on pushing on with the meeting for both the purpose of landing a contract and getting more information if it was to be had.

"While I get the sugar-free dessert plated, I did want to congratulate you again on the Grilling Association recognition. Second runner-up is still great publicity for the restaurant. I see you put the trophy here in the private dining room with some of your other awards. Did you go out and celebrate after?"

"It was a Saturday night. No head griller who owns a restaurant goes out and parties. By the time I got back to town, I went home and went to bed. I left Angela in charge on a busy Saturday night knowing I'd be coming in Sunday morning to clean and do all the prep for Sunday. Mackenzie, you know what Sunday is like, right?"

"I do. Busier than Saturday for me. If I don't pace myself on Saturday, Sunday is awful." She now knew that Brandy had no alibi, but did she have a motive? As she served the final dessert, she listened.

"Apparently, Bobby was so hyped up about winning, he didn't have a care in the world what happened at his restaurant on Sunday. He already had Jason to cover Saturday night. Guess he just thought he could take the weekend off. I can't remember the last time I had a weekend off." Clearly, she resented Bobby, but it didn't seem like enough to commit murder. "Did I mention he also stole all of my sauce recipes when he hired Jason?"

"Bobby stole them?"

"Yeah. Bobby started using my sauce recipes after he hired Jason. Bobby wasn't going to actually change the menu or do anything that might risk his precious family-business image, but he suddenly had decent sauces for everything. Then miraculously this is the year he wins Griller of the Year. Color me shocked!" There it was. Brandy felt like she had been cheated out of a higher place in the competition, and he had Jason who brought along her recipes to help him. Even if she didn't want to date Jason, clearly, he was an asset.

"Well, what did you think about the dessert choices?" She got what she was looking for and now she needed to seal the deal on the business transaction. "Would you be interested in setting up an arrangement for purchasing desserts from my shop to serve in your restaurant? I'd be happy to put business cards or flyers in my shop as well, recommending you to my customers."

Brandy still seemed distracted, thinking about Bobby and Jason, but responded to the questions. "Yes, but can we try it for two weeks and see how they are selling?"

"Of course. You'll need to gauge how much you need and how often so you're not overbuying and so you're only using fresh products. If it has my name on it, I only want you to be using the desserts when they are at their highest quality.

They all shook hands with Mackenzie and agreed to order pie, cake, brownies and the sugar-free option starting Friday night as Mackenzie would need to bring in extra supplies to fill this new demand. Secretly, she hoped Brandy was innocent so this deal would continue. As she drove the borrowed Volvo back to her house, she considered all of the information she had on their three suspects and what she and Arthur would do now that they seemed to be at a standstill. Quitting now sure would be a mis-steak.

Chapter 9

Put a Fork in It

MACKENZIE AND ARTHUR SAT IN HER LIVING ROOM, debating what their next move should be. It was getting late on Wednesday, and they had three suspects with motives and no alibis. She felt as if she was in no better position today than she was Sunday morning.

"Are you feeling like maybe we just need to hand over the information to those State Troopers and be done with it. Maybe something we know will help them in their investigation and it won't be all for nothing." Mackenzie's tone showed she was clearly getting discouraged.

"Well, that's not a bad idea. Maybe we can have a conversation with them, and they might say something that helps us. Most likely, what you said is the best-case scenario. If anything, we found can help them, it's best to share the information now and not wait. The longer an investigation like this goes on, the less progress there is to be made due to less and less new evidence."

Mackenzie took out the card Officer Zhào had given her just three days ago. Arthur was still in the room while she made the call but couldn't hear what was being said on the other end. When she hung up, she rotated her head to the side and sighed. "Guess where they want to meet?"

"Hopefully the bakery."

"We're not that lucky. They were coming into town to talk to Jason again so they figured we could meet at Porter's, if it wasn't too much trouble. Ugh! I've seen enough of that place for a whole year."

"What did you say?"

"Of course I said we'd meet them there."

Two hours later, Mackenzie and Arthur were walking together to the end of the Cozy Cove peninsula to take a seat at Porter's Steak House. It took about ten minutes for Officer Zhào and Officer Smith to show up. "We're very sorry to be late. It took longer to leave our previous engagement than we expected."

"No problem. We're just happy to let you know what we know and see if it helps. Any chance you've made any progress?"

"Well, we have a little information we didn't have Sunday morning, but that's about it," Officer Zhào hinted.

Mackenzie leaned in a little and waited. She hoped they would share a tidbit, a morsel of information, she didn't already know.

"Upon examination of the body," started Officer Smith, "Bobby was found to have a large piece of glass in the wound. It was a triangular shape and appeared to have broken off inside his body."

Mackenzie pondered this fact. She had a feeling, like a word on the tip of her tongue she just couldn't spit out.

"Does that ring any bells, Ms. Walsh?" Officer Zhào was now the one sitting, silently waiting for new information.

"I can't figure out why, but it seems like a puzzle piece I've been missing and now can't place."

After everyone sat for a minute or two not speaking, Mackenzie and Arthur proceeded to share what they thought to be motives for each of the three competing chefs. The troopers took notes and asked the occasional question, but nothing really seemed to excite them.

"Maybe we should ask Jason and Heidi the questions we have so you two can enjoy the rest of your night. We know you work in a bakery, so you must need to get home soon."

"We've been burning the candle at both ends this week, so it's become par for the course."

Trooper Zhào waved to get Heidi's attention.

"How can I help you?"

"We'd like to speak to the chef. If you could make that happen, we'd be grateful. We just have a couple questions for him."

"I'll see if he's available."

"Please do and thank you."

Heidi scurried off through the door to the kitchen. Jason followed her back out. She must have told him which table because he was headed in the correct direction immediately.

As soon as Jason arrived tableside, he asked, "Officers, what can I do for you?"

"Jason," began Officer Zhào, "we know you were working the night Bobby was killed because he was at the award ceremony and the restaurant was still open."

"That is correct. No one really asked me any other questions because I clearly had an alibi. The rest of the kitchen staff too. Saturday night was hopping, and without Bobby here, we had all hands on deck."

"And was Heidi here too?"

"I probably only saw her once or twice the whole shift because of how busy everyone was. By the time I went to leave, everyone else was gone. I locked up and went home to shower and pass out, luckily in that order." He chuckled like the joke was much funnier than it actually was. "You'd have to check with her to see what time she left."

"We will. Thank you." After a slight pause, Officer Zhào continued, "Did you have any reason to murder Bobby Porter, other than getting to take over his restaurant?" That would be leading the witness in a court of law, but with a rock-solid alibi, they could say most anything to get what they needed from Jason.

"Look, Bobby rescued me when I thought I might be done in restaurants. He really believed in me, and I felt like part of a team for the first time in a long time. No, I didn't want him dead."

Officer Smith asked, "Do you think anyone else wanted him dead?"

"I think plenty of people have had the thought 'I'd kill for...' and you fill in the blank. I just can't imagine anyone actually killing Bobby."

"Jason," Mackenzie interrupted the dialogue between Jason and the troopers. The three tablemates stared at her. You could have heard a pin bone from a salmon filet hit the floor. "Have you found the award that Bobby won yet? Has anyone located it?"

"I haven't seen it or heard anything about it. Why?"

"Officers, I'm pretty sure if you can find the award Bobby won Saturday night, you'll have found your murder weapon." Arthur was the only one whose face reacted with realization instead of confusion.

"Jason, can I borrow the newspaper clipping from Saturday night off the wall?" Mackenzie pointed in the direction of the front door.

"Sure. Heidi," Jason hollered across the dining room. "Can you grab the newspaper clipping and bring it here?" It really wasn't that far and Mackenzie would have gladly gotten it herself, but this was even better than she could have hoped for.

Heidi walked across the dining room to the table where Mackenzie and Arthur sat with the two state troopers.

"Heidi, did you work all night Saturday night." She looked confused. Well, I worked until we stopped seating new tables."

"And did you call Bobby from the restaurant Saturday night?"

"I can't remember. Why?"

"Officers, you did get phone records for Bobby's cell phone, correct?"

"Yes. And there was a call to the restaurant, but we didn't think much of it. Where are you going with this, Ms. Walsh?"

Mackenzie looked at Arthur, who nodded in agreement.

"Arthur and I suspect that you'll find somewhere in Heidi's car or home the rest of the award he won Saturday night." Mackenzie pointed to the award Bobby was holding in his hand in the newspaper photo. The base appeared to be stone, in the black and white photo it was tough to tell, but the rest was glass in the shape of two flames. The awards won by the other three chefs were small and had one small glass flame, but Bobby's was much larger with two distinct flames, presumably because it was for a grilling award.

"That's a pretty big accusation you're throwing around, Ms. Walsh. Do you have any facts or evidence to back that up?"

"Well, based on what you just said about the glass in the wound, I believe the top of his award was used to stab him. See how there is a second smaller flame? When I discovered the body with Lucas, I noticed some bruising or damage to the skin on one side of the open wound. I think this is what stopped the flame from going in even deeper and possibly why it broke off."

"That is an amazing hypothesis. Anything else?"

Heidi stood in stunned silence. Mackenzie might have imagined it, but she appeared to be backing up ever so slightly.

"Arthur and I have been trying to figure out who had the most to gain from Bobby's death. The obvious answer is Jason."

"Now, hold on a minute. I was here, working. Everyone saw me until late in the night. Even then my doorbell camera will show what time I got home. I didn't have anything to do with this."

"I don't think you murdered him, Jason. However, someone else would benefit from Bobby's death that led to your promotion. You and Heidi have been dating, have you not?"

"We were trying to keep that quiet. It's hard to run a restaurant if the staff thinks you are playing favorites."

"Well, with Bobby gone, Heidi secures her job and also secures her new boyfriend a position as head chef instead of sous chef. I'm also going to bet the two of you, together, spoke to his family about buying the restaurant, eventually anyway."

At this, Heidi started to run toward the front door. Officer Smith, being the one closest to the fleeing suspect, jumped up and was able to grab her before reaching the podium. "Heidi, you are under arrest. Anything you say can and will be used against you in a court of law..." Officer Zhào moved to assist Officer Smith as they walked her out of the restaurant, completing her Miranda rights along the way.

Arthur looked to Jason and then Mackenzie. "How did you put it all together."

"It came down to motive. While all three chefs had a motive, they just didn't seem strong enough for murder, except maybe Mark Dunn. He was my top suspect for most of this. If Porter's had closed before the publication of that magazine and Well Dunn moved up the list to first place, it could have made a huge financial difference, as well as possibly allowing him to buy this property. Jason, will you stay on without Heidi?"

"Absolutely, but I'll need to hire a new front of house manager, so changes may have to wait a little. I can't believe Heidi would do such a thing. We were together, but it wasn't that serious yet."

"I'm going to guess it was that serious for her. Just be glad it wasn't you that ended up dead."

Jason swallowed and considered that scenario. "I guess you're right."

"I think we're all done for tonight. We have a bakery to run in the morning and a new contract with Brandy Kelly to sort out."

"You're working with Brandy? How?"

"She signed a deal for two weeks to buy desserts from Top O' the Muffin to Ya to serve in Respect the Skirt. Are you interested as well?"

"I may be interested. Let me know at the end of two weeks where you stand. I'm not interested in stealing you from her, but if she doesn't want the deal, I may take it."

"Sounds good. I don't think we'll be needing dinner tonight, and I'm guessing the troopers won't either. They have some unexpected paperwork to do now." Mackenzie looked very proud of herself. Arthur looked proud of her too. He smiled as he nodded slowly.

"Well, I'll get back to the kitchen. Don't forget to contact me in two weeks. Good night."

"Good night." Mackenzie and Arthur walked out of Porter's just as Heidi was being driven out of the parking spot in the back seat of the troopers' car.

"Arthur, what do you say we go home and get some sleep. That was a busy start to the week, and we still have a full weekend coming up with new desserts to supply on top of our regular business."

"And you still have a meeting with Brian to look forward to."

He was right. The day had been so long already, she forgot Brian had taken the photos just this morning for the postcards.

"Well, I guess I do."

"I feel badly for Heidi that she was desperate enough to commit murder and now she'll probably spend the rest of her life in jail."

"You know what they say?" Arthur winked at Mackenzie. "That's the way the cookie crumbles."

"Oh, Arthur."

Recipe

Cranberry-Orange Muffin Tops

Ingredients for muffin tops:

1 cup all-purpose flour

1 3/4 tsp baking powder

1/4 tsp salt

1 large egg

1/2 cup granulated sugar

1/3 cup Greek yogurt

2 TBSP freshly squeezed orange juice

1/4 cup canola oil

1 TBSP freshly grated orange zest

1 1/2 cups fresh cranberries

1-2 TBSP flour for cranberries

Ingredients for topping:

2/3 cup all-purpose flour

1/3 cup granulated sugar

1/2 tsp cinnamon

1/4 cup unsalted butter – melted

Preheat oven to 400°F. You can use flattened paper liners in a muffin top pan or forgo the liners.

For topping, in a small bowl, mix flour, sugar and cinnamon. Add melted butter and mix with a fork or fingers until crumbly, and place in the fridge until ready to use.

For muffin-top batter, in a large bowl, stir together flour, baking powder and salt and set aside.

In a medium bowl, whisk together egg, orange zest and granulated sugar until just combined. Whisk in yogurt, orange juice and oil – mixture should be pale yellow.

Fold wet ingredients into dry ingredients and whisk everything together.

In another small bowl, sprinkle 1 1/4 cups cranberries with 1-2 tablespoons of flour and toss them gently until all berries are coated with a thin layer of flour and fold them gently into the prepared batter.

Spoon batter onto muffin top pan indents, without spreading the batter out to the edges, filling about 2/3 of the space. Cover generously with streusel topping. Place a few extra cranberry halves on the tops of each muffin top if desired.

Place filled muffin-top pans in the oven, and reduce heat to 375°F. Bake about 15-18 minutes or until the toothpick inserted in the center comes out clean.

PLEASE LEAVE A REVIEW!

★ ★ ★ ★ ★

Virginia K Bennett

An Appetite for Solving Crime

THANK YOU FOR READING MY BOOK!

I WOULD LOVE TO READ YOUR FEEDBACK ON
FACEBOOK, INSTAGRAM, AMAZON, OR
SIMPLY SEND AN EMAIL TO:

authorvirginiakbennett@gmail.com

About the Author

When she's not writing on her couch with her two cats, Twyla and Geo, Virginia is busy teaching middle school math, grocery shopping, cooking or spending time with her husband and son. Together, her small family loves to go geocaching and visit theme parks.

Mysteries have always been an interesting challenge for Virginia, much like watching a magician perform. Unless you want to hear the entire thought process behind who she thinks is the killer and why, you might want to avoid watching any movies together.

The path to publishing a book is different for everyone and her path is full of twists and turns. Thank you to those who support the journey.

facebook.com/AuthorVirginiaKBennett

instagram.com/authorvkbennett

Printed in Great Britain
by Amazon